For Darcy,

my very own grumpy Gus.

First published 2020 by Macmillan Children's Books
an imprint of Pan Macmillan
The Smithson, 6 Briset Street, London, EC1M 5NR
Associated companies throughout the world
www.panmacmillan.com

ISBN 978-1-5098-5436-3 (HB)
ISBN 978-1-5098-5437-0 (PB)

1 3 5 7 9 8 6 4 2

A CIP catalogue record for this book is available
from the British Library.
Printed in China

Merry Christmas
GUS

Chris Chatterton

This is Gus.

Gus doesn't like
Christmas.

Gus doesn't like Christmas decorations.

He doesn't like Christmas carols.

HOWWLLLLL

And he doesn't like
scratchy Christmas jumpers.

Gus doesn't like it when it snows.
He doesn't like silly snowdogs.
And he certainly doesn't like . . .

...MISTLETOE!

Gus really doesn't like Christmas at all.

But maybe . . .

. . . Christmas isn't just about what Gus likes.

Maybe Christmas is about doing things
for those you love the most.

Even if you are
a bit grumpy.

Perhaps Gus could like Christmas decorations, jumpers and trees if it meant spending more time with me.

We like
Christmas games.

We like
Christmas feasts.

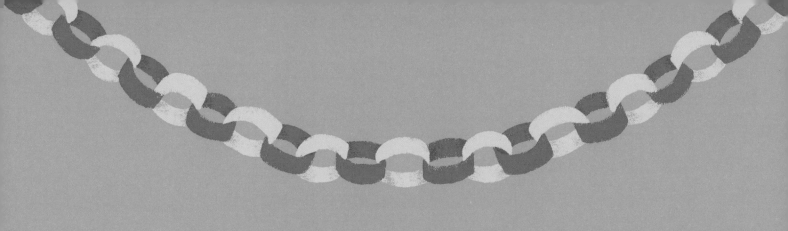

Now Gus loves Christmas
just as much as me.

But Christmas isn't the same
now there are three.